SECRETS FROM THE

Secrets from the Red Phone Box

Philomena Plunkett

YOUCAXTON PUBLICATIONS
OXFORD & SHREWSBURY

ISBN 978-1-913425-58-6
Published by YouCaxton Publications 2020
YCBN: 01

YouCaxton Publications
www.youcaxton.co.uk

For my brother Richard who left this planet too soon.

Contents

SPIRIT OF THE ICONIC RED PHONE BOX REVEALS ALL

I REMEMBER WELL the first person to make a phone call from my phone box. You always remember your first time at least that's what I heard someone say in my phone box on many occasions. Like your first love you never forget.

It was a man. How do I know this I hear you ask? After all I am the spirit of the red phone box. I can hear voices, hear conversations by deep listening, only one side of course, and whatever is said in my phone box stays in my phone box. That was always my motto but now I have decided to reveal all that went on in and around my phone box. I can pick up sounds and hear voices if they are within 100 yards of me, even further if the wind is blowing in my direction. I am working hard on developing my other senses, sight might be some years off but, I can hear the sound of paper and am registering every minute detail when people talk about pictures and letters. Touch is coming along nicely although I can't physically touch people I am touched by the amount of joy and suffering that has been expressed over the years in my box. I connect with the sound when humans bang my door or rest their bicycles against me. I register this as touch feeling, but it has yet to penetrate my box.

Yes I am on the edge of discovering human feelings. I do know when I or others are happy, sad, or lonely. My biggest fear is I may be turned into an emotional wreck with all the stuff I am picking up from humans who come in here. I am not sure the ability to be emotional is all it is cracked up to be.

The day I made the distinction between male and female

voices was when a group gathered outside my phone box. There was a humming sound like bees in a hive, I was straining to hear what was going on when a shrill, plummy voice arrived and said, "Good morning ladies, welcome to our annual trip to the Chelsea Flower Show, for those who don't know me I am Pauline Wallace, president of our local Women's Institute (WI), I will be joining you today."

With that, I heard muttering sounds exclaiming how disgusting a particular man was. Someone said, "That is Reggie Wordsworth, he is so rude! Just look, he nearly knocked Felicity down."

Apparently, Reggie had shoved his way through the group to get to me (phone box), I was pleased but the group were not amused. Then the gossip started, and they laughed at the way he dressed and gave a full description of him.

"Just look at his flat cap and plus four breeches. Someone should knock him down to size and make those breeches fit, landed gentry indeed, they think they can ride roughshod over the rest of us," said Gertrude.

Then a timid voice said, "They often dress up like that when they are going to kill innocent animals. Look at this red, whisky nose and very large belly, watch how he enters the phone box – he has to turn sideways."

Dotty pipes up and says, "The only nice thing about him is his grey hair, long grey beard and moustache in the shape of bull horns, I do like a well-groomed man."

Reggie bolted into my phone box, pulling the door shut said out loud, "Bloody glad to have this phone box to save me from that mob of females." As the women boarded the bus they made a sound which was as mesmerising as the sound of a starling murmuration and then peace was restored.

Poor old Reggie, I am glad he feels safe in my phone box. Little does he know I think his voice is dull and monotonous, sometimes I would just tune out of his conversations. The females expressed the notion that he would get out of his Land Rover often leaving the engine running with absolutely no consideration for the environment, while he popped in to use the phone box, like he used everyone else in the village. Every Friday at 2pm without fail he would phone the cattle market to check how well his animals were doing, what price they fetched etc., I often heard him ask if they achieved the blue badge this week.

He was so boring, I often thought his conversations would be more interesting if I could hear the person on the other end of the phone but that was not possible. Reggie would keep saying, "No, no you fool! I just want to know if they achieved blue!" It was only over the course of his conversations that I found out 'blue badge' was some kind of approval for the high quality of your animals at market. He was obsessed with the colour blue.

I usually stopped listening while he talked, so 2pm on Fridays became my nap time. My ears pricked up when, out of the blue, he started coming into my phone box saying, "I have to wait until 7pm to phone this one, I don't want her old boy to catch us." I was listening so hard I was picking up the lowest of the lowest frequencies which was consuming a lot of my energy, but I was curious. I became interested in his conversations because his voice had changed, there was a bit of excitement and rhythm coming from him. I knew most businesses would be closed at this time so conversations must be of a more personal nature and I really liked this.

Blue was definitely the theme of the conversation as he would say, "What are you wearing? What colour are they?" Then there would be a long pause and he would make heavy breathing noises down the phone. Sometimes he would laugh and say, "Little boy blue has lost his shoe" and gently replace the receiver in its cradle. I gave him the benefit of the doubt when I heard this, thinking maybe it was his shoemaker he was talking to. So many times, I wished I could hear what the person on the other end of the phone was saying. I was intrigued and my evenings began to liven up although I was getting concerned for him each evening, he was adding more and more words to the conversation and his breathing was getting more agitated. Then one dark winter evening he came into the phone box and started with the same question, "What colour are they?" Suddenly I heard some crashing, banging and dull moaning sounds coming from the lower part of my phone box. I was powerless to do anything. It was not until I heard the clatter of the milk bottles and the milkman stopped, pulled old Reggie out and made a phone call asking for an ambulance. The milkman said, "No he is not breathing, he is stone cold and is blue all over, I think he is dead." All sirens wailing and screeching the ambulance and a police car arrived. This really added a bit of excitement to my otherwise quiet village life although I thought it was quite sad, I will miss old Reggie.

SCHOOL'S OUT

THE VOICES OF children are a mixed bag, ranging from soft and gentle to squeaky or shrill – high-pitched, demanding, repetitive, penetrating tones. Damn! I hate children. I used the word 'hate' because it is a word I hear most often from the children. I have picked up this fashionable expression from the kids, "it is what it is" this seems to bode well with me, like "I hear what I hear and nothing else."

Therefore, I can't say I hate children, that is not my word but they are quite annoying and amusing at the same time. Especially the little red-haired kid, his name is Richie E, I heard his friends call him this. They also call him many unpleasant things when he is not around and to be honest, I have to agree with them.

He is a leader, with charm and authority able to order his friends to do silly things. He even has the audacity to call my phone box his HQ. I would not mind but his hair is not actually red. His friends joked and laughed when they discussed the colour of his hair saying red is the colour of the phone box; you are more like orange, carrot colour. I am glad he is not like my red box – if only I could talk, I would kick his tiny ass out of my phone box. He and his gang meet in here every evening after school if it is not already occupied. Sometimes they have to be hauled out by the ears by adults who need to make important or emergency phone calls.

One day there were five of them all squeezed into my phone box; they had come in after football and Tom said the smell was putrid, it was worse than Mac's farts and they were so rotten even I, who has no concept of smell, could imagine it.

They were planning a secret mission to stop old Mr. Peabody – the maths teacher – from giving detention to the girls. Peabody did this on a regular basis and was often seen in the girls' changing rooms after school. Once, when he was approached by some of the boys, he said he was tidying up, if they did not want detention also, they should leave immediately. The boys suspected him of being a sleazy pervert. They decided to make an anonymous call to the head teacher pretending to be one of the parents. Richie E elected Ollie Snot (his real name Ollie Macintosh) to make the phone call. His voice had broken, and he was the geezer to do it (not my words), I wish schools would expand children's vocabularies.

The boys had a system going; you could earn points for each dare carried out and whoever had the most points by the end of the year was elected to assistant leader.

The red-haired kid was the leader and once you got to be leader there was a two-year term with benefits. The leader got to make the final decisions, and everyone paid a 5p membership which the leader got as payment for keeping the gang going. Much to my annoyance they also got to keep any change that could be extracted from the phone coin box by constantly bashing it or pressing buttons. If you banged it for long enough money might drop out or someone might have forgotten their change. Sometimes they could take up to a pound from me.

The school was about 200 yards from my phone box and the kids would pass by every day. In the mornings they did not have time to come in and pester me. The afternoons were horrendous. If there was an adult making a phone call the kids would circle around the phone box shouting and banging on the door often blowing bubbles with their gum or stick it on the window. Winter time or rainy days were worse, often the phone box would get all steamed up and the kids would breathe heavily on the windows and write all sorts of obscenities, vile words most unbecoming for children. One little fellow wrote, "I love Missy" and the bigger boys made fun of him slagging him off for weeks, this was not considered cool, although it had my vote.

In addition to the redhead's HQ, my phone box also played host to the redhead and his friend Joey, a fat kid who was not a member of the gang – had their own tricks to play. They had a habit of ringing up various businesses in the area playing practical jokes on them. There was a very funny one, even I had to laugh at this when they pulled down the Yellow Pages. Sifting through the book, they decided on funeral directors, standing on the book to reach the coin box they dialled the company and asked to speak to Myra Mains, all I could hear was giggling from the two boys and they left, leaving the Yellow Pages on the floor.

They were not bad kids really, in fact most of the time I really enjoyed their company. It was all very innocent, and their call to the headmaster about Peabody actually had a very good outcome. Peabody was suspended from duty for three months and when reinstated he was not allowed to be left alone with the girls or give them detention.

MY TALENTED FRIEND

I LOVED TAMARA Paige and her dog Jasper, she was my new literary friend. I seem to be getting more cultured individuals in my phone box now. She uses me as her office, a far cry from Red's gang although I will always love them. One hot summer's evening she came down with Jasper and read out loud to me her first-ever story she had just won a short story competition in the local literary magazine and wanted to run it by her Uncle Sean who lived in Scotland. I could hear her counting out all the money – it was not cheap to make a call to Scotland.

"Hi Uncle Sean. Yes I called it 'There was a noise'. I don't have a lot of money for the call so I will try and keep it short." Then I heard the phone being put down. That was quick. I could hear her breathing and she said to Jasper, "Good boy I won't be long."

Then I heard my phone ringing. I do like the sound of it and Tamara said,

"That is so kind of you Uncle, reversing the charges. I will keep it brief," She then began.

"The title is 'There was a noise'. I hear it now. Listen can't you hear it? On good days, it sounds like the chorus from Madam Butterfly, that beautiful humming noise that can send me off to sleep. It smells like jasmine floating in the summer breeze. It tastes like chocolate ... soft and sweet that lingers long after it has gone.

"On bad days, it sounds like rain bouncing on a metal roof. It smells like pigs wafting in the wind. It tastes like marmite, the food I hate to eat. There was a noise I hear it now! If it were a dance, a tango it would be. Intense, captivating, intriguing and mysterious but no one understands. There was a noise so frightening it left me traumatised for many years. I hear it now, the sound of broken glass as I am propelled towards the front windscreen of my car. Lying there for what seemed hours, hidden in the ditch behind a tree that had come down. Jasper, my dog, is scratching and howling on the back seat. Worried about him I slur my words trying to reassure him that all will be fine. His constant yapping keeps me from going into an unconscious state. We will be OK Jasper, someone will be along soon. I see headlights coming towards me. I think I am shouting loud enough but like a candle in the wind it dwindles and everything goes into darkness. Jasper limps into the front seat and sits on my lap providing much needed heat to my body that is slowly growing cold. I can feel his hot breath on my face. I have no sense of time. The clock on the dashboard no longer works –

the time is set at 1.20am. As I drift in and out of consciousness losing hope that we might be found, I hear a noise, the sharp pain in my neck prevents me from seeing what is going on. The impact of the crash seems to have heightened my senses. I can smell them, the childhood memories of little piglets come to mind, but, peering through the glass I see some snouts pressed up against the window; they come in search of food but could that food be me? They are no longer little piglets with curly tails – they are giant boars. I panic, thinking of stories of how pigs can eat humans or worst of all eat Jasper my lovely dog.

"I say 'postman' to Jasper and he howls like a wild beast up against the glass, his saliva is streaming down the window like rain and the pigs retreat. I try to press my head against the glass but cannot, I know it is close but yet it seems so far away. I see red in the reflection of the glass, crying hysterically I apologise to Jasper for having got him into this mess and sorry that he might be bleeding. The blood was coming from me, my nose was bleeding, I could feel it trickling down my throat, the taste so bad it reminded me of marmite.

"I am so, so, sorry Jasper, if I die I want you to know I have always loved you. I remember when I got you from the rescue centre, you popped your little head through the bars and wanted me to take you home there and then. When I explained I could not and I would be back after the home checks were done you whimpered and seemed to understand. I could not sleep that night. I sat up praying to God that you would not be taken by anyone else. I asked Daddy that if I went to bed earlier would Friday come quicker? He tried to reassure me saying of course it would but I had no need to worry because he had signed the paper and handed over lots of money for you. Once Friday came you would be a new member of our family: me, you and Daddy, we were a great team.

"If we are not found tonight we might get to see Daddy sooner than we expected and we both howled so loud I did not hear the noise. It was the light that blinded me – the flashing police cars, torches glaring through the window. Jasper and I were airlifted to the nearest hospital; there was a noise, the whirling blades of the helicopter.

"In the air ambulance they placed you on my lap. I heard the doctor say, 'It was the dog who saved her life keeping her warm and conscious with his body heat and his constant howling.' Two years on the road to recovery I can say there was a noise but I can no longer hear, taste or smell it. It is slowly fading.

"Thank you Uncle Sean, I am so glad you like it. Love you too."

Tamara had certainly educated me on what a noise might be like, that one could digest it. I might never have the pleasure of the sense of taste but I will always be grateful to Tamara for enlightening me.

MR. LUCY – MUMMY'S BOY

EVERY FRIDAY NIGHT Mr. Lucy would pull up outside my phone box, lean his bicycle against me and dig into his pocket, pulling out a little brown purse that contained money. He would lift the receiver and dial the operator, he had to call his mother who lived in Dorset, she was now 80 and she still controlled his every move. He never married. Two females were gossiping outside my box and one said that when Lucy's father left home for another woman, the mother used emotional blackmail to keep her son from leaving her, threatening to commit suicide if he ever left. He had been working away from home, renting a room with Ms. Therese in Harebell Cottage, just next to my phone box, for a year and had to phone Mother every night. He had been coming to my phone box for almost six months now and to be honest he is so tedious, "Hello Mother, hope you are well. Yes, I am fine, of course Mother." Then the beeps would go, and he would sign off.

WHAT A TRIUMPH

IT IS A cold and windy day, and no one has come to make a call. I hope nothing serious has happened, not another war or disaster. Just as I thought that, I heard boys whistling, making hooting sounds, expressing oohs and aahs and saying, "Wow! Look at those wheels! It is a Triumph Spitfire, don't see many of them." They circled round the car for closer inspection. Then one chap said, "Forget the wheels, check out the blond she is girlfriend material, with the figure! She looks like some film star, not many of them around here either."

"Excuse me I have to make a phone call, you can sit in the car, I will take the keys with me." I could hear them jingle as she walked towards my phone box. "I might even give you a ride when I am done."

Then I hear a noise, the sound of shoes stepping into my phone box. Not the usual dull sound but a click-clacking sound. After hearing the description of this wonderful lady, I am curious as to what conversation she might have to offer. Then she caresses the wall behind the receiver, reaching into her handbag, pulls out some sticky tape and places paper on the wall. She left without uttering a word. I am left feeling a little disconnected and disappointed, I might never know what is on that paper, my sight is not developed enough to read it. When the door closed behind her I heard her invite the boys to take a lift with her and the sound of the car engine drifted in the wind.

SCHOOL PICK UP

ANOTHER SCHOOL DAY and for once I am willing the redhead to come into my phone box. He comes up and is lingering by the door, swinging it open and shut. Is he coming in or not? I am pleading with him to come in. I really want to know what the notice says. Then he runs after Ollie and says he can't meet up today because he had to do a mega job, top secret, for his big brother.

His job was to pick up his little sister from school but that would have made him out to be such a sissy in the eyes of the gang. He had this amazing ability to be creative when he needed to.

THE UNWANTED BABY

I GATHER HOPE as someone enters the phone box, I can hear rustling of papers and lots of sniffling sounds. I struggle to hear her. Oh no! She is crying. I hear the receiver being bashed about, the ding of money drops in the empty coin box and she says, "About time, I thought you would never pick up. I don't believe it Marie, I am pregnant, and the father does not want to have anything more to do with me. He now tells me he is married, and I must get rid of the baby. I am so scared. I just don't know what to do."

I am left feeling speechless. I am powerless. I can't do anything. This is not what I want to hear. There is no way I can expect her to even notice the sign when her life is in such a mess. She leaves, saying she will visit the clinic tomorrow and arrange for the termination. I am left feeling really sad.

THE CHILD CARER

I COULD DO with some good energy vibrations after this female left my box. Well, jolted out of my deep space I hear a voice say, "Hello Kevin, shouldn't you be at school?"

Then my door opened and Kevin was talking, making muffling sounds. I could hear him breathing as he said, "Mind your own business fat face."

Hearing the sound of coins rattling was my cue to listen in.

"Hello? Hello? Is that Social Services? I want to speak to Mr. Jones with regard to my parents."

"OK. I can hold on but not for long, I am phoning from a phone box and don't have a lot of money."

Then there was silence I was not sure what was going on.

"Hello? Have you forgotten me? Hello? Hello? God, I hate this stupid music."

"Ah yes. It is Kevin Smith, you said to phone. I need help. Dad needs care now that he is in the wheelchair and Mother too. No she can't help, you know she is blind and can't do much.

"I am doing my GCSEs and I have to have some help."

"Oh no! Don't put me on hold again.

"If only they knew the half of it, not only do I have to cook, wash and shop for them I have to make calls to the betting shop for Dad which I hated at first, now I am getting to really enjoy it. I often put a sneaky bet on for myself, I know it is illegal but there is nobody to care what I do."

Then I could hear a tapping sound.

"Oh yes! I am still here. Yes, I am doing my GCSEs and need support. OK that would be useful. Yes I will come in for a meeting. Yes 20th July, I'll just write that down. Yes, someone to come in two days a week would be really helpful."

Then I heard a bashing sound as the phone call ended. Everything goes quiet, the silence is broken by my favourite sound ... the ding of coins. I never heard Kevin leave, maybe he is making another call.

"Hello?"

His tone of voice is slower and deeper than before.

"What are the odds on Bletchley Park running at Cheltenham, 2 o'clock this afternoon? I'd like to put on a pony each way."

His conversation is not making sense. The last time I was confused about conversations was a long time ago. Men often came into my box using words like GCHQ from time to time. I overheard people say they were government agents from the Secret Service. They were fascinating conversations once I got familiar with the codes. Top secret, of course, I could never disclose them to anyone. Kevin said he was doing GCSEs and asked to speak to Social Services – there must be a connection as it sounds similar, GCHQ and Secret Services.

"No, I want to place a bet on another horserace."

Maybe he is a secret agent because Martin Farrell, a regular to my box, often puts £10 on a horse to win at Cheltenham. I still don't understand what it is but over the years I have become quite knowledgeable about some animals and sports.

Jessie Whelan is always phoning the Pony Club with information about the latest events, I often heard her say a pony was far better than a horse because horses were used for hard work and racing competitions while her pony, although it had four legs and was a similar animal to a horse, was smaller and for important posh little girls only. So why is Kevin putting a pony on a horse each way?

"Sorry just hold on. I have to put some more money in."

There goes the best sound, the ding of coins dropping in.

"OK now I want a Lady Godiva to win on Nelson's Column, charge to my card, code number 69453, Name: Handcock, and OK got it. 'Bye."

Now I am totally confused and will have to wait for his return to try and decipher his codes. There was a rapping on the side of the box and I heard a man say, "Don't pick your nose and leave it on the phone, other people have to use it." Kevin left with the same words he entered, "Mind your own business, fat face."

NEW LIFE

THERE IS A lady in my box, she reminds me of Reggie. She is talking to her friend on the phone saying she had to enter the phone box sideways. "Yes, the baby is due today. That is why I am phoning you, I need you to get home as soon as possible. I need you to be with me, I can't do this alone." Then I hear the phone hit the wall. "Oh no, it is coming! I can't have my baby in a phone box, hurry send an ambulance. I'm at the village green phone box!" I heard screams like I never heard before – they went from high to low, all coming from the young lady.

I can't do anything for her. Oh No! Someone come quick, I can't bear the sound. Then the familiar sound of police sirens and lots of voices saying, "It's OK, you are in good hands." Whispers turned to gasps of joy and then a sound I never heard before, like crying, squealing or wailing and a policeman said, "Congratulations, you have a beautiful baby boy." The sound of a new baby will be forever embedded in my phone box.

People flocked to the phone box after that. The local newspaper came to take my photograph. I think they said I was a celebrity or something to that effect. I did not understand what the lady meant when she said, "It was a great story, first baby to be born in a phone box; nearly as good as the baby who was born in a stable." But I loved the tone of her voice.

THE IRISH EXCHANGE

I HAVE GROWN to love the Irish accent. It is soft, mellow with a lilting melody that can make a sad story more acceptable. Paddy O'Toole is a regular visitor to my box. He is staying in a caravan site just over the hill at the end of the village where all the Irish workers live while building a new bypass. I believe this is a road that will link our village to an important town and one can get there in less than an hour. I hope this does not encourage people to take their calls away from me.

A few of the Irish lads come in to ring home. Paddy makes most of the calls. I am not sure if they have Irish women as they never come in to my phone box. Paddy is the leader of the workmen. When he rings home he often says just tell Mrs Brown and the news will spread like wild fire though all the villages in Ireland, a bit like a news reporter and, of course, it saves money. I heard him say to his mammy, "The phone boxes here are the same as the ones in Ireland only they are a lovely red colour. However, you can't beat the green ones at home." I am not sure why he would want to beat them and hoped he would not want to beat me.

He often says he needs a break from all the emotional pulls the gang put on him. He is seen as a hard man. I heard one of Paddy's workmen say, "Paddy O'Toole is the hardest man I ever worked for, a big man with a short temper, a real Jekyll and Hyde. He could knock a man to the ground if he was not behaving or doing a job right while at the same time rescue small animals. One day we were just about to pour some hot tar down when he spotted a hedgehog in the middle of the road. He actually halted the job until the hedgehog was put safely into a nearby hedge. When all is said and done he is really a big softy. I think his bladder is located too close to his eyes." I later learned that this meant he cried a lot.

Today, he is phoning his daughter in Australia with some news, "Hello Kathleen. I am fine, are you sitting down? I have some very sad news. Your mammy is not very well, no; no I mean she died last night. Kathleen, can't you find it in your heart to come home for a bit? I know she said some terrible things to you before you left." Then there was a pause as Paddy pulled the receiver away from his ear.

"Yes, I know, what she said, if you did not come home when she was alive not to come home when she died. She only said this because you broke her heart leaving, not just going to another country but to another continent, to go all the way to the other side of the world, after all she had done for you, and taking her only grandchild. Can't you forgive her, isn't it time to let bygones be bygones?

"I thought you, Kathleen were different, belonging to the new generation where holding a grudge was no longer the way of things. My generation would get great mileage out of holding a grudge but you know it did more harm than good, particularly to the one holding it." Just as conversation was getting very intense the beeps started to go, I hope he has some more money I want to know more.

"Christ! Hold on Kathleen! I need to put more money in." Then I heard the ding of coins. "OK, I will hold you to that. The funeral is on Saturday so two weeks after I will pick you up from the airport. I must go now. I am returning to Ireland myself tonight, I love you Kathleen, see you soon."

I could hear the sound of silence as Paddy held onto the receiver then breaking the silence he cried like a baby for what seemed like an eternity. A big strong man like Paddy needed a place to release all his sorrows. I wanted to help but I was powerless. I never did know what Kathleen's mammy was called as Paddy always referred to her as Mammy.

FREE PHONE CALLS

I HEAR A storm brewing, heavy whistling winds rustling through the trees, a crackle of lightening and thuds of thunder here and there. I don't imagine many will be out tonight. My door is bashing back and forward. The roof is leaking – must be the cracks where the paint is peeling off. I heard a man say it was looking bad and would need some repairs.

The rattle of milk bottles brings me back to life and the milkman makes a call, "Yes, the power lines are down, and I can't get through the village this morning, I will have to come back later." He leaves shortly after this, and then I heard two men in my phone box saying, "Let's get on with this job, we don't have long and there might be a lot of people using the phone because of the storm and we have to make it look like we are proper maintenance men doing repairs." I can hear loads of clipping noises and chat about how they are going to fix it. I have no idea what is going on. Then the guy called Ajoke says, "No one will suspect us here in this sleepy village."

I am not sure what they mean, is it something to do with the notice the lady put up? "If we move these wires and disconnect this one, we can then make calls all over the world without any cost to us." So, they continued to do the work and suddenly I hear them talking in a language I have never heard before. I want to scream for help, I will even be nice to the red-haired kid if he comes by.

"Great Ajoke, good job, let's get out of here." I am totally confused, first the notice, now people speaking in strange languages. Then everything goes quiet. It is now morning and the phone is actually ringing, what is going on? This has never happened before. It rings and rings then it goes quiet. It is now 8am, I only know this because the milk truck has gone by, has done for the last five years at the same time. I get this odd feeling people are coming from all areas, people I have never heard before. Someone enters my phone box and starts making calls. I have no idea what they are saying, the only word I recognise is 'Nigeria' but I don't understand the language. Then a queue begins to form all the way down the village high street. One after the other they enter my phone box, make their call and leave. The only noticeable factor is they are not paying for the calls because I cannot hear the ding of money being slotted into the money box. I have been violated, the two that came in yesterday must have disconnected the payment system and now everyone is taking advantage.

I am overwhelmed by all these strangers and miss my little redhead. I can hear him at the back of the queue, every day for the last four weeks. I am willing him to come in, but he can't get past the crowds, then he starts an argument with some of the bigger boys, but they beat him up and the police arrive. The police gathered statements from everyone, and it turns out the phone had been rigged up to allow free phone calls. This was happening all over the country. If it was not for the redhead no one would ever have known.

Red is taken away in an ambulance. I hope he is not hurt. Weeks pass and the gang don't meet here. My time is spent thinking about him and hoping he is OK. I had forgotten about the poster on the wall, somehow it did not seem to concern me anymore.

FINALLY THE NOTICE IS READ OUT.

PEOPLE COME AND go, nothing terribly interesting is happening. If I could feel something, I think it might be low energy. Nobody is surfing the sound waves – I need people to engage with me. I think I might be like Mr. Lucy, sad I miss Red and the gang. Late one evening Mr. Lucy shows up resting his bicycle against the phone box. He dials the number and waits anxiously for his mum to answer; she seems to be taking her time I do hope she is well. He looks up and sees the notice on the wall. Reading it aloud he says, "Seats caned phone Silvia, all calls taken in the strictest of confidence." I wonder why it says 'in confidence' if you are only getting your seats upholstered. Then he says, "Yes, Mother, it is me. I am fine, are you well? OK, good night Mother." He replaces the receiver, reads the notice again and the next minute I hear him ask, "Can you tell me what your service is please? Great, give me your address, I will call tomorrow."

This appeared to have put Mr. Lucy on the path of no return. When he came in the next night to phone his mother he said, "Hello, Mother. No, I will not be phoning you tomorrow or any other night for that matter. Goodbye."

After that notice was read out my phone box took a turn for the worse. A man came by and put up more signs, as he made bashing noises he exclaimed, "I wouldn't mind meeting some of these skimpily clad ladies I think I will keep some of these pictures for myself." Women came in sticking posters of everything from ironing services to French lessons. It was hard to know what was going on. Were these advertisements a euphemism for something else? Yes, don't be surprised I can use big words; remember I was created by well- educated stock! It was all down to Mr. Lucy, he was my regular informer reading the signs out loud, laughing and saying I wonder what mother would think!

ABANDONED

PEOPLE HAVE STOPPED coming into my phone box, they pass by carrying objects up to their face and have plugs in their ears. I am not sure what is going on. One very wet day I heard a noise, someone hops into my phone box! They begin having a phone conversation without using my phone. The person said they had just got a new iPhone. Typical of people these days, an iPhone is all about me, me, me, no regard for others. "I can't believe how fantastic it is and I will never need to use these horrible, ridiculous phone boxes again!" I screamed, "Get out, how dare you!" but they could not hear me.

Redhead has left school now and the gang have all grown up and gone away, I do miss their visits. I have had the odd person drop in and when I say 'odd' I mean it in a weird way. To my horror, one odd person used my phone box as a toilet! I heard someone say as they opened the door, "Oh no! Someone has pissed in here, how disgusting." A couple were in here for ages in the early hours of the morning, they whispered most of the time so I had no idea what they were up to but there was a lot of rustling and moaning and groaning. I waited anxiously when I heard the man say, "I am going to put it in now." I waited and waited but did not hear the ding of money in the coin box. I guess I will never know what they were doing.

To add insult to injury, British Telecom came and ripped out my phone communication system. It felt like they ripped out my heart. Keeping a very British stiff upper lip, I remained strong and kept my spirits up for the sake of the phone box. The weather is not kind, it is stripping me of my paint and the hinges on the door are going rusty. The door that would spring open, allowing people from all walks of life into my phone box has not been used for some years now.

THE IN-BETWEEN YEARS

I MISS ALL the chatter. The voices that often offended or annoyed me, I longed for. My door has not opened in a very long time. Have you ever heard the sound of silence? Not sure what is going on, just when I had entered the land of silence, I heard a smashing or shattering sound and a voice said, "You idiot, you broke the glass of the phone box, run quick."

I wanted to say, "Please stay! I don't mind really! Please come back and stay a while." But no, I only heard the sound of heavy feet making a retreat.

Word must have gone around because Mrs. Tate (from the manor house) began to check up on me from time to time. Often talking to her dog or friends outside my box, she would say, "We must think outside the box about what we are going to do with this great piece of British engineering."

Sometime after the glass was broken I heard screeching sounds, very high-pitched then low and raspy sounds. The noise increased, as time went on I had no idea what it was. Thank goodness for Mrs.Tate! She popped in with a male person and they were discussing putting a new pane of glass in the box. Then the screeching noise began again. Mrs. Tate stopped talking. I felt really sad I wanted her to talk for ever. Suddenly she said, "Johnny look over here, it is a robin's nest! Look, two little eggs."

"How do you know they are robin's eggs?" asked Johnny. "Well I am a bit of a birder and robin's eggs are pale cream or buff colour with tiny red specks, known as eggshell blue. They can lay up to five or six eggs at a time, unfortunately many don't survive and the sparrowhawk often eats the eggs or the young."

Then the male voice said, "We certainly must delay fixing this window until the birds have flown the nest, conservation and RSPB guideline you know. As soon as they hatch and fly away we can put in the new pane of glass."

This made me very happy when they explained everything. Next day, Mrs. Tate came by with her grandchildren. "Gather round children. Be very careful, don't touch the nest. Soon these little eggs will hatch and the robin family will have two beautiful baby chicks. Come along now, we must not disturb them." The door closed gently as the Tates went home.

I don't want the birds to go. They are attracting so much attention, bringing lots of people back to the old box. When they sing I feel alive again. My box has been empty for far too long. It is not the same without sound. I became accustomed to the sound of the robin, then one day I heard the tiniest crackling sound which reminded me of the gang, when Ollie split his trousers, a tearing, ripping sound. Then the chirping of the birds got louder like there were more of them.

Mrs. Tate arrived again with the grandchildren. Taking the

nest down she showed the children the empty eggshells saying the robin family had flown the nest with their two little baby chicks. They used the phone box as their hatching space and would not be returning. I was so proud and pleased to have had them on my patch.

"They will not return so now I can put the new pane of glass in. Come along children, we can see what the nest is made of. Tiny twigs, strips of bark from the tree, feathers and, I do declare, some dog hair, moss on the outside and lined on the inside with soft feathers."

The children were so amazed that birds could make such a home for their family just by using their beaks. "Please Nanny can we come again? Could we turn this into a hospital for stray animals?"

"Great idea George but not sure it is big enough or we would get planning permission. I was lingering onto the sound of their voices as they left my box. I was not sure I would ever hear them again.

When the man came to fix my window I really enjoyed the sounds he was making – smashing and bashing, really bringing me back to life again. Then people started to come in and out for a short time. One man came in shouting at the top of his voice, "Someone robbed the telephone, damned vandals I will have to report it to the police."

Then I heard coins rattling, such wonderful sounds. "How am I expected to report this crime when there is no phone in here?" Then I heard a loud bang and a tender female voice say, "Come along now Mr. James we must get you back to the home."

Mrs. Tate arrived to check the repairs to my box. I am growing very fond of her. Talking to her dog she said, "Goodness, one thing after another, look boy moss, nettles, and fungi growing in the corner. I really must take them out, although they do look pretty and I can bring Sophie and George down next week to see them." I became very upbeat when she mentioned there was some fun guy living in the corner. I really needed some fun, just like the good old days when Redhead was such a fun guy.

I heard Mrs. Tate say she knew someone on the council and was owed a favour so planning permission was not going to be a problem. I will just telephone them and we should have the notice up within a few weeks. I have had some opposition from two influential people in the village but I will sweeten them up. I will get Polly, my cook to rustle up a banquet at my house then they will be putty in my hands, she tapped the side of my box and left.

To my horror I heard someone outside my box saying, "I must put my glasses on and read this notice, can't imagine what they are going to do with this now. I won't be too disappointed if they tear it down; it is beginning to look like an eyesore." After the rattling and rustling in the bag, I heard the female voice say, "Brilliant, marvellous! They are going to turn it into a library. A font of knowledge in our own little village." I can't tell you how excited I was to hear this ... me going to be a place where people can seek knowledge.

As people stopped to read the sign outside my box it was music to my ears because they would stay and chat – most were very complimentary indeed.

RESCUE

ONE DAY, TWO ladies came into the empty phone box taking measurements and discussing what they might do with me. One lady said people have mobile phones now and have no need for me, that my phone box weighed approximately 600kg and was 8ft tall or 244cm. They laughed hysterically, saying imagine anyone walking around town with this phone box up to their ears. Technology is moving so fast it is important to preserve our heritage, "hear, hear, I could not agree more" and Historic England is putting a preservation order on all red phone boxes. I was very relieved to hear that. Then the other lady said, "Yes, villagers can now adopt a phone box, a scheme taking over the maintenance of each phone box." I do hope someone nice adopts me and it does not take forever. I have been privy to many conversations about adoption and I believe it can take years.

I am sad and I just want them to leave me alone to try and comprehend all this change. They left and a few days later I heard Mrs. Tate marching down the high street. Shouting at the top of her voice, "We got planning permission, all systems go. We can now get on with our plans for the library."

I am very excited, little Mrs. Tate from the manor in the village has summoned a posse of individuals and keeping to the planning permission was turning me into a library. She also championed the colour of the phone box to remain red and I was now given the royal warrant of a Grade II listed building.

I was concerned that a library would be too quiet, I would miss all the gossip and nothing much would be going on. I need not have worried, it was 26th July and notices were up around the village announcing the opening of the new library. Not content with calling me old, she has now suggested I was going into retirement and would become a library for the village people.

Mrs. Tate and her gang of volunteers were down the night before, stocking the shelves with all kinds of books. All the books were donated by the villagers – there were fiction, non-fiction, travel guides, cook books and autobiographies, it gave a great insight into the minds of the villagers. All those years of deep listening have really paid off my senses are being educated to a higher level I am beginning to get a handle on what it might be like to be human.

The sun was shining, and Mrs. Tate had brought pot plants to decorate the outside of the phone box. She made a speech that seemed to go on forever which I quite enjoyed as I knew it may be the last voice I might ever hear in my phone box. I welcomed Mrs. Tate and used her as a trusted conduit to relay my story. So, when she says "I" she means me, King Red of the phone boxes.

THE SPEECH

WELCOME, I WILL start with the brief history of the red phone box that we have all grown to love, a symbol of great British Architecture and engineering. In 1923, the Royal Fine Arts commission ran a competition with entrants from the great and good putting forward designs for a telephone box to house a communication system that would allow the ordinary public across the United Kingdom to make telephone calls in comfort. The results were very disappointing, so they got the top brass to get involved which included the Royal Institute of British Architects, Town Planning Institute, the Royal Academy and the Postmaster General. Finally, they got the Royal Fine Arts Commission to organise a limited competition and invited only three titled men, the leading architects of the day, to enter.

The outright winner of the competition was Sir Giles Gilbert Scott, he had just become a trustee of Soane's Museum and was well connected. Sir John Soane was an English architect who specialised in Neoclassical design. He came from a very humble background, as the son of a bricklayer he went on to become a professor of architecture at the Royal Academy and an official architect to the Office of Works. He received a knighthood in 1831. The reason why I tell you this is Gilbert's design is based on the dome of Sir John Soane's mausoleum which can be seen in St Pancras Old Church Garden, London; it is a Grade I listed building.

I, red phone box, for the record am officially a Grade II listed building. Go on, tell them that Mrs. Tate, and she did! "If I had my way, I would have them install a communication system at the mausoleum so we could try and talk to the dead." I could hear the surprise in Mrs. Tate's voice as the words spirited out of her mouth; remember I am in control of this speech. I had found a voice and was going to use it to my advantage. After all, I had been a listener for far too long. Tell them about the King's part in this and she did. "It was thought the people of the country should be allowed to have a copy of this fine phone box, so thousands of little red phone boxes were made and shipped out to all corners of England to celebrate King George V's Silver Jubilee in May 1935."

I tried to influence Mrs. Tate to talk more about my history and noble connections, but people kept coming up to her and saying not to drag the speech out much longer.

"I won't go on much longer but I think it is important to mention that the red phone box began life as K1 and as each design was modernised it went from K1 to K8, each time making it more affordable." Then I interjected to tell them a joke, and she said, "I think they stopped at K8 because it was thought if they had a K9 (canine) it might encourage people to bring their dogs in, and I certainly did not want dogs coming inside the phone box, it was bad enough that they should mark their territory outside the phone box which happened way too often. Anyone with a keen interest in these amazing phone boxes can see and compare two fine examples, K2 and K6, located on the high street of St John's Wood, London."

Mrs. Tate's best friend, Fifi Hunt-Taylor laughed and said, "I don't know what she is on about, Gladys loves her dogs, think she has been on the sherry earlier than usual this morning." Then the vicar interrupted carrying a huge bunch of flowers ran over and thanked Mrs. Tate for her amazing hard work and constant contribution to the village.

"Thank you one and all for coming today, I now declare this library phone box open," and with that Mrs. Tate cracked a bottle of champagne over my box. Ouch! That hurt. Fifi said I am so glad the old girl did not crack the real champagne and used the cava, save the good stuff for us to enjoy later. I wondered would it have hurt less if she hit me with the champagne instead of cava? I guess I will never find out.

It was a great day, I was able to tune into the voices of the villagers and hear some good gossip, I soaked it all up. The vicar said, "May we have a rousing round of applause for Mrs. Tate, hip, hip, hurrah! Please feel free to take a look inside and join us for afternoon tea which will be served in the vicarage, everyone is welcome."

I heard Matty Tinker, the local blacksmith, say to his friend that she forgot to mention the crown motif that was put on the outside of the phone box to represent the British Government in 1926. Personally, I think some of those phone boxes might have been bugged trying to capture spies and with that I lost the thread of the conversation as they moved on to the vicarage. I began to feel sad as everyone drifted away. I thought about the wonderful individuals who entered my phone box and wondered whatever happened to them.

Day-to-day visits were non-eventful. I missed the young people. It was not until the Spring of 2016 that things started to pick up.

After the wonderful speech and all the voices that entertained me that day I was ringing, the ringing is only a memory but that is how I describe my excitement at what was going to happen next. Would Mrs. Tate visit more often?

Time was passing. I got used to the sound of my door opening and closing, crackling sounds and even the low frequencies of pages turning. I knew you were going to ask how I recognised the sound of pages turning. I heard a flicking sound one day and a female voice said, "Hey Dave, you would love this, it is a real page-turner." And the same clicking noise started again and the Dave person said, "You're right Annie, thanks."

There was huge excitement once when a female voice said, "I don't believe it! Look! I found some money: a one-pound note in the pages of this book 'How to enrich your soul.' I am going to go through all the books now and see if there is any more money hidden in the books!"

I could hear bashing and banging, vibrations that were not particularly good ones. This went on for ages. "Just my luck, nothing here and I am certainly not going to tidy this place up, I just got some paper cuts – I best get home quick and disinfect myself, never know what you could catch from old books."

The door banged and I heard nothing for a long time. Suddenly, I heard Mrs. Tate in the distance. I have tuned into her breathing system, I can hear her coming before she arrives. The sound pattern often changes, sometimes, there is a heavy breathing sound followed by a thud, thud, thud. If it had been anyone else it may not have sounded so melodic.

She always makes some reference to how she is feeling when she gets to my box. Things like: I am not sure how long I can keep this up or I feel wonderful today, glad to be alive. I wish she would make up her mind.

When she said, "I must not run, it is not good for my breathing or my heart, I can hear it beating so fast," I wanted to say I can hear it too but I could only register those sounds for now and loved the sound of her heartbeat.

Upon arrival she said, "Tulip we must clear up this mess. That woman who found a pound-note in the book must never be left alone in this box again and while I am away."

Oh no, don't go away, don't leave me.

"Pay attention Tulip, this is no time to be doing your meditation and airy, fairy yoga practice. I need you to listen up. I will be back in five weeks (I was very relieved to hear her say she would be coming back) and I need you to look after the books here in our lovely phone box, make sure it is clean and tidy."

When a response came I was somewhat surprised by the light high-pitched voice drifting in and out like a loose connection. Riding the waves of this tone I try to register the word 'Tulip', my register only knows the word tulip as a plant. Someone once said, "I love tulips. I plant tulip bulbs every year and they pop their colourful heads up through the earth with such strength and determination from the underworld – a sure sign of Spring."

This could be interesting. I am being left in the care of something that comes from the underworld. Please don't go Mrs. Tate but I was reassured when I heard Mrs. Tate's voice drifting away, "Remember Tulip, look after the books and, of course, the box, it is very special to me and the community."

I wanted to say the same to you but she could not hear me.

No activity for a while until I heard the sound of barking I have become accustomed to the sound of dogs over the years. I like a good loud bark, it is more preferable to me than whimpering, whining sounds and the added addition of humans saying, "Shush, shish, I won't be long."

"Stop Fanny, good girl wait."

It was The Plant that came with Mrs. Tate yesterday. Bashing, scratching and singing sounds started. It took me a while to separate the sounds but in the end they all sounded like bashing.

There was a wonderful sound which reminded me of the old days; a ding similar to the sound of coins dropping into my box. I was so enjoying this until I heard The Plant say, "Good girl, thank you Fanny for being so, so, good allowing me to clear the energy in the box. Now it will have positive vibes and the old bad spirits can be banished forever."

What is The Plant on about? I wanted her to go and leave. I needed the spirits of the past to stay, they are what made me. If only I could talk, I would tell her to get the hell out of my box now.

The rattling and the singing continued, "Oh Buddha you're so fine, you're so fine you blow my mind, hey Buddha."

"Look Fanny, don't you think the Buddha statue looks good here, OK let me turn it slightly to the left so people passing will see it. Make the box more appealing to everyone."

How dare she try and upstage me with a Buddha! In my phone box not sure what a Buddha is but if Tulip is organising it, it is bound to be odd.

"Doesn't it look amazing Fanny? Now I can organise the books. Hmm! Not a lot of meditation or enlightening books here. I shall bring my personal selection tomorrow.

For now, I will put Alan Titchmarsh alongside 'How to cook with Floyd'. No better still, look, a Fanny Cradock cookbook. I will let them snuggle together on the shelf until I bring my vegetarian and vegan books next time."

I wanted to scream which I have not done for some time and say, "Get out! And don't come back!"

I could hear the door open and close, thank goodness she must be gone. Then the sound of a dog whining and whimpering like it was never going to stop. I realised The Plant must have left the dog behind. I could hear the thud of feet getting closer and the sound of the door opening. The Plant said, "Ooh, ooh Fanny darling, Mummy was such a mindless nincompoop! I would never leave you behind all, accompanied by the sound of slurping and sloshing."

It did not seem long before The Plant was back again muttering, making the most piercing sounds as she shuffled in my space. After a lot of noise she said, "I wish this box was bigger. It is fine to sit and meditate in but not suitable for yoga, I couldn't possibly do downward dog in here." I don't hear her dog, Fanny, so I am not sure what she is talking about.

In a wave of excitement I had a strange sensation come over me, no it can't be The Plant from the underworld trying to enlighten me whatever that means, whatever can it be? My vibrations are getting stronger and stronger, something familiar is happening. This only ever happens when Mrs. Tate is around and I am sure she is still away. Maybe she is not that far away, I can definitely hear her breathing.

Excitement registers when my lovely Mrs. Tate arrives although not sounding her usual delightful self, the sweet lady I remember. I do hope she has not changed while she was away. I remember someone say that when their beloved daughter returned from being away in an Ashram in Indian she was a completely different person. Maybe that's what happens when one goes away.

"What on earth are you playing at Tulip? Are you out of your mind putting a statue of the Buddha in our phone/library box? What would the Vicar say? Take it out immediately. Remove all the Buddhist books from the top shelf, you may leave one or two, we need a variety, this is not a Buddhist Temple." I was cheering her on, you tell her Mrs. Tate and tell her to keep her Fanny under control. That was one of the best times I have had for a while all thanks to Mrs. Tate getting rid of the Buddha and The Plant.

SOLVING A MYSTERY

TWO PEOPLE PASSED my phone box, now library box, and intimated that the night was glorious with a full harvest moon, so bright you could read a book under it. Later, I heard voices saying, "You idiot, why are you wearing a hat and sunglasses? I could have lent you my balaclava." I heard them whisper, "I can't see a damned thing with these sunglasses, maybe you don't actually need them." I know I am a phone box but wearing sunglasses at night is very unusual, unless of course one is blind. Oddly enough, by this person's actions, they could be blind as they are making so much noise. They slipped into the phone box and removed magazines from under their coat, leaving them in the corner on the floor beside the travel guides. I hope they have permission from Mrs. Tate. After that night a constant flow of young boys and men began to enter my library box which I thought was very unusual. They would reach in, take a novel from the top shelf and then reach down on the bottom shelf and roll up a magazine, stuffing in down the leg of their trousers or shove it inside their sock.

It was Craig from the village pub who gave me the lowdown on what was happening; he brought his friend down and explained the system. "Right, you just pretend you are taking a book from any shelf and make sure you are holding it up where people can see it when you leave the box. Then you reach down for the magazine and stuff it somewhere under your coat." "But what if I don't have a coat?" "Use your loaf," said Craig.

There were comings and goings, but the silence was eating away at me. No one was making conversation. I did not know what was going on. Mrs. Tate arrived to clean the library phone box. I loved it when she visited, she always talked to herself or would sing a song. She really brightened up my day. She would wash the windows. I really enjoyed when she used her feather duster to reach the top of the phone box, it made me feel a little giddy as she tickled parts that had never been touched before.

Duster in hand she shakes it around, slapping it down heavily on the spider's web, the duster flew out of her hand landing on the magazines. Then I heard, "Oh my God. What on earth is this?" I tuned in very quickly. I recognised this tone of voice from the old days when people came in to make phone calls. It was of grave concern and shock.

Then I heard Mrs. Tate's angry side, "The dirty scum, soiling my beautiful library with porn magazines, I will get to the bottom of this." I was getting very excited, porn magazines in the village library! I am not sure why I am so excited because I don't know what porn is. Whatever it is it was getting me and Mrs. Tate energised and that had to be a good thing. Then she sat down and flicked through the magazines, trying to figure who might be responsible. I thought she was looking for evidence, but she lingered over certain pages longer than others.

Thinking out loud she said, "I will have to lie in wait and try and catch the offenders." This was not surprising as she had donated most of the first four shelves of detective novels in the library. When she stopped talking, I thought if only I could speak, I could tell her what I heard.

She started to hang out at different times of the day; talking to herself she began to investigate some of the suspects. Vicar Brian was a regular to the library, always taking out her detective novels so he was beyond repute and, of course, a man of God.

Could it be Lady Brown from Bartram Hall? She did look the part, a bit like a porn star – you know the sort, big boobs and plastic surgery that was beginning to sag, she did hang out with very risky individuals. Or could it be Farmer Egan? He did live on his own, never married and could be the type to indulge in porn magazines.

Weeks went by, I wanted to tell her to go down to the pub because Craig knew what was going on and maybe he could help. But I could not speak. Then to my delight, Mrs. Tate had a meeting outside my box with Sabina Barac, speaking very quietly she said, "Sabina, this is in the strictest confidence I tell you this. Yesterday, Sammy was doing his paper round when I was pulling out of my drive, I narrowly missed knocking him off his bike, his satchel and all the contents went all over the road.

"I jumped out of the car, checked if he was OK and bent down to pick up all the papers, insisting he come inside and get his breath back. He went into the bathroom and while he was there, I searched through the contents of the satchel. Lots of newspapers and a magazine wrapped in white plastic, I examined the address on the package, and to my horror I saw Vicar Brian, The Rectory. I held it up to the light and there was the latest porn magazine.

"Not wishing to cause alarm, I quietly tucked the magazine down the side of my sofa. Made Sammy a cup of tea, gave him his satchel back and when I thought he was ready sent him home. If this scandal gets out, they might close down the library, I might be seen unfit to adopt the red phone box. What is really bad, if the Vicar is reading porn magazines, what would the congregation think? I went to see the Vicar he invited me in, explaining that he had not put the porn magazines in the phone library, but his rooms were broken into last week and lots of things got stolen. It may be the young pranksters from the village had put them in."

"Your secret is safe with me darling, good luck with the Vicar, I am off now, duty at the church is calling, 'bye" said Sabina.

Then the door opened, and the voice of Mrs. Tate said, "I am so sorry that this has happened to the most amazing red phone box ever to grace our village." She sang as she cleaned the library, going through every book exorcising all the demons from her beloved library.

Then the Vicar arrived head hanging low. With a quivering voice he said, "Mrs. Tate, or may I call you Gladys? I want you to know I have cancelled my subscription, I ask for your forgiveness."

"Glad to hear it and Mrs. Tate will do for now."

After the clean-up and make-up of Mrs. Tate and Vicar Brian, Mrs. Tate was left alone with me. I know I am a phone box, but my senses have become very acute over the years. I have developed a deeper sense of feeling. I think Mrs. Tate with her cleaning instruments and happy disposition has stirred my emotions.

In that moment I nearly cracked under the weight of Mrs. Tate's (or Gladys's) little speech. She said out loud, "If this phone box could talk, I am sure it would tell many a fascinating story. We have had births, deaths, affairs, children's pranks, every human activity has happened in this box. Although it is a small library with books on the shelves, the invisible stories that are written into the fabric of the phone box may never be told and will remain the secret of the phone box." I wanted her to know I could hear her, I wanted to say, "I love you Gladys and thank you for adopting me!" but she could not hear me. I do believe she felt me when two books fell on her head and she screeched, "Ouch!"

VILLAGE NEWS

THERE IS TALK in the village that an invisible virus is attacking vulnerable people to the point of actually killing thousands around the world. I fear I might be a target because I am the invisible listener in this area. Will they find out my secret; hunt me down; maybe actually remove me? After all, I have so much information about everyone that ever used my box. I have to be rational about this no one actually knows that I can hear them or that I was developing strong emotions for Mrs. Tate.

Nobody actually died when they entered my box. This is not entirely true. Reggie died all those years ago, right here in my box. If they remember this they might start blaming me. I am not sure what a virus is but I heard it is deadly and everyone will have to social distance until they find a vaccine. The presidents and governments of countries worldwide are advising their people to stay home.

Suddenly I hear the door open someone was coughing and sneezing and making moaning sounds. "My hands are so cold, I do hope the snow stays a little longer it makes the phone box look so pretty."

When I hear compliments like this I want to be all sloppy and emotional again. No, stop! I must remain objective during these difficult times.

The voice started again. "Oh, look a good book about Presidents of the USA." Then I heard the turning of pages and the voice started again.

"Shame they don't have an up-to-date book about that orange Trump fellow that recommends bleach and takes drugs to ward off the virus." I am excited it was like old times, my energy started to pick up. I was curious I wanted to know more.

I immediately thought he might have been talking about Red from the old days. Remember? Red was not actually red he was more orange, maybe Red went away to the USA and became president but he didn't drink bleach or take drugs, he was a sensible chap, so it can't be Red. The coughing began again and the male voice said, "Ah this will do 'The Planet of Apes' always a good book to escape into." And he left.

It was not long before I heard the sound of cars pulling up and the lovely Mrs. Tate's voice. No, stop thinking about her in this way.

"I am sorry but it's orders from the council," said a male voice, "we must not have this library open, every other business is going into lockdown. The virus can spread so easy on door handles and on books. People coughing and sneezing in such a confined space, it's the droplets that bounce around everywhere. Really sorry, Mrs. Tate, but it will help stop the spread of this invisible virus."

I am invisible and perhaps they think I am the virus, I am not sure what a virus or a vaccine is but they seem to think I have something to do with it. Why else would they be going to close me down? Maybe they will do some horrible experiments on me or send me off to the phone box graveyard.

There was a ripping sound, like Ollie ripping his trousers; only the sound was at least 100 times louder. They left all the books inside and sprayed the box with chemicals." This spray will kill

99% of all germs, even the President of the USA recommends it." said Mrs. Tate

"Ah, 99% that sounds right as there is one germ still running the country and he is orange," said Jim from the council.

When they left Mrs. Tate said, "I am so sorry Bertie." And she patted the side of my box; I never knew she called me Bertie, such an affectionate name I really like it.

She stood back from the box and said, "The red tape is really not that bad looking, lends a bit of sex appeal. Don't worry Bertie? I will think of something to get you out of this mess, we won't have you gagged for long."

For the second time in my life I have been gagged, my ability to be of service to the community has been taken from me. First was when they took out my telephone system, now the library. But I have faith in Mrs. Tate, she rescued me the first time and she just said she could do it again.

The sound of her footsteps retreating brought sadness to me although I trusted her implicitly – I was not sure about anyone else. "You know trust in a person is the highest quality in any human being" so Molly Bán says.

I went into involuntary isolation or social distancing as people outside the box said when they stood one metre to my left and one metre to my right using me as a barrier. So once again I was of use to the community and this really pleased me, it gives me a great sense of duty when I can be a help to others.

For a time people did come by and peeped in through the glass, saying as soon as this virus is gone I am going to go in there and get that book. Then no one came by and I missed the sound of voices. Not even nature could penetrate my box as they had put so much tape around me. The blackbird was my lifeline, it kept me alert as it sang twice a day.

There was part of me that was in denial, I did not want to believe this was happening. I was left with my memories of the past which kept me going for a while. I was luckier than humans. I was used to being alone although I did depend on people for interaction and it was during those moments I felt most alive, I was glad in a way that I was in control of my emotions and did not develop the full range of human emotions. I was able to observe how I was becoming dependent on Mrs. Tate. I understood only too well about making connections and disconnecting from conversations, it can leave you all up in the air this happened with much frequency when I operated as a phone box.

Time goes on and people pass by without even peeping in. Have they forgotten about me? Fortunately, it did not affect me the way it affected humans. I heard someone outside the box say they were so grateful to all the villagers how they rallied around and helped each other.

There was a coordinator called John who organised a band of volunteers to collect prescriptions from Boots, the chemist, often having to queue for hours outside keeping the two-metre distance. People began to talk much more to each other as they took their daily exercise. Some saying they never did exercise before and this was a great time to stop and reflect on what was important in life.

I loved getting a drift of conversations. I might equate it to how a human's spirits can be lifted by beautiful acts of kindness in simple gestures of a smile, a wave, or just a nod to someone who might be in a deep place of suffering.

I heard Mrs. Tate arrive. I felt we were more on business terms now as she began to unravel the tape from my box. She had Tulip with her, how things had changed. Mrs. Tate said to Tulip, "I want you just to listen to me and please don't answer back, this is a very important job. I want you to take a good example from the phone box Tulip, the success of our operation today depends on you just being like a telephone/library box, listen only to the instructions and be silent at all times. We don't want a repeat of your last visit, understand Tulip?" There was silence.

My energy had been fuelled, I was slowly coming back to life with the lilting sound of Mrs. Tate's voice. I was delighted that she silenced Tulip, but what were they going to do?

Mrs. Tate gave instructions to Tulip explaining what she was to do, this was like music to my ears. Like the good old days when the sound of coins dropping into my box had the feel-good factor.

"We will pack the books and store them in my garage until this dreadful lockdown is lifted. Take this antibacterial spray and go over the whole box Tulip." They spent hours cleaning my box, every inch, nothing escaped the cleaning hands of Mrs. Tate and

Tulip was an exemplary assistant. "We will leave the door open, put that brick as a door stop, we don't want people opening and closing the door, they can just peep in, you know how curious people are."

Then she began to fill it with flowers. "Look Tulip someone has knitted little figures of doctors and nurses to honour the NHS, a mark of respect for the selfless work they have done during this dreadful time. I just can't imagine the strain the Hospitals are under, every single care worker from the medical staff to the cleaning staff, and all in between, of course, the volunteers working to save lives." Then she cried. Tulip went to say something but Mrs. Tate said, "You know Tulip I don't do public displays of emotions but this virus thing has really got to me. Don't tell anyone one I cried, I need to be just like the phone box and keep a stiff upper lip and be a support for those that need me, together we will fight this."

I wanted to say I hear you Gladys feel free to cry in my box your secret is safe and I am here to listen.

TELEPHONE
PUSH
BREWERS

Printed in Great Britain
by Amazon

68756547R00041